The Shiniest Rock of All

The Shiniest Rock of All

NANCY RUTH PATTERSON

Pictures by Karen A. Jerome

AN AUTHORS GUILD BACKINPRINT.COM EDITION

The Shiniest Rock of All

AN AUTHORS GUILD BACKINPRINT.COM EDITION

Published by iUniverse, Inc.

Special thanks to Whitney Matthews,
Luke McCabe, and Beverly Thagard, who knew Robert first,
and to Pam Feinour, who made Chunkie climb the mountain

iUniverse books may be ordered through booksellers or by contacting:

iUniverse
1663 Liberty Drive
Bloomington, IN 47403
www.iuniverse.com
1-800-Authors (1-800-288-4677)

Originally published by FARRAR/STRAUS/GIROUX

ISBN: 978-1-4401-1620-9

Printed in the United States of America
iUniverse rev. date: 1/20/09

For Dorothy M. Hannaford
and the Martins—Gene, Judy, and Beth
—N.R.P.

To Mom and Dad,
for always being there
—K.A.J.

and Ian,
your great aunt Susan
and Uncle Dean join me
in wishing you a very
merry Christmas.

[illegible] Ruth Patterson
2010

Contents

The Shiniest Rock of All

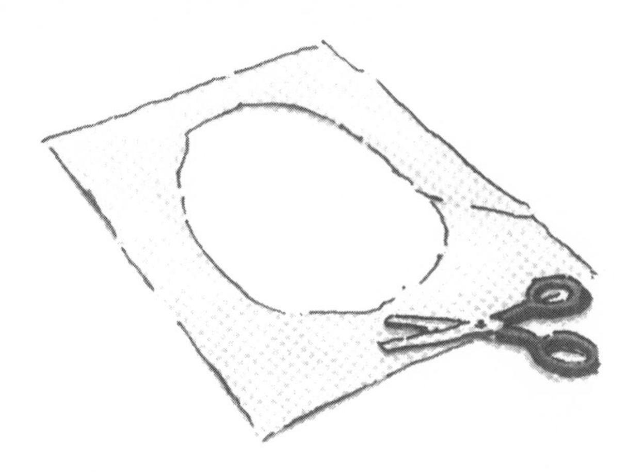

"Twick-o'-Tweat"

"Robert Morris Reynolds!"

Robert absolutely hated his name.

He liked the Robert part, after his grandfather, who had been a catcher for a minor league baseball team. He liked the Morris part, too—it was his mother's name before she was married. And the Reynolds part, his father's name, was a name to be proud of, Robert was often reminded. His father was a judge in Clarkston, Virginia, where they lived.

So it wasn't exactly his name that Robert hated. It was the way it was said. This time his mother was saying it, and she was saying it loud. And she followed his name with the words "You get in this house this *instant*."

"I think you'd better go," his best friend, Mike Evans, said. They were up in Robert's tree house.

Robert had just traded Mike one Dave Winfield baseball card for one of Ozzie Smith, a trade that would give Robert all of his favorite Cardinals.

"Robert, I said *now!*" his mother yelled.

Robert picked up the card and stuffed it into his hip pocket.

"I never go the first time she calls," Robert said to Mike. "If I did, she'd think I'd done something to be worried about."

But Robert didn't wait for his mother to call him a third time. He jumped the eight feet from his tree house to the ground while Mike climbed down the ladder.

The two walked through the backyard to Robert's house. Robert gave Mike their secret best-friend handshake, which changed from week to week. This week, it was two long squeezes followed by three short ones. Then Mike ran to his house around the corner.

Robert kicked at piles of fallen leaves. He tried to guess what his mother had found out about this time. True, he and Mike had smashed the Millers' pumpkin last night on Halloween, but nobody was there to see them do it except Ronnie Pendergrast, and he never squealed on anybody. So it couldn't be that. His room was clean, if you didn't count the dirty socks and underwear stuffed under the mattress. But he'd been careful to push them near the middle of the bed, safe from his mother's eyes. So that probably wasn't it. And report cards didn't come out until later. So what was it, he wondered. What was his mother hollering about this time?

"Robert Morris Reynolds!" his mother yelled through the kitchen window. "I said this *instant*!"

Robert quickened his pace. He caught the swinging back door to their Victorian house with his foot before it slammed behind him. His mother was scraping carrots at the kitchen sink. That was a good sign. Mothers who are furious do not usually pay attention to dinner. Then she slammed the carrot down and turned toward him. Robert wished she hadn't slammed the carrot down. That was *not* a good sign.

"Mrs. Snead called me a few minutes ago," his mother began. So that was it. Mrs. Snead hadn't been on Robert's top-ten list since last spring when she got him in trouble for kicking a soccer ball through her kitchen window when the garden club was meeting in her living room.

"So?" Robert asked. It was better not to tell his mother anything she might not already know. The less said, the better.

"She said you hissed and spit at her last night when you went trick-or-treating," his mother said.

"I did not hiss and spit at Mrs. Snead," Robert said slowly.

"Do you mean to stand there and tell me that Mrs. Snead would call and tell me something that wasn't true?"

"I didn't spit at Mrs. Snead . . . and I didn't hiss at her either," Robert repeated.

"Then what exactly did you do to her?" his mother asked.

Robert thought for a minute. Then he blurted out, "I sizzled."

"You what?"

"I sizzled at her. I went trick-or-treating as a fried egg, and I sizzled when people answered the door."

"Robert Morris Reynolds, I'm ashamed of you. You left here for the Halloween party dressed as a ghost and you know it. I cut the holes in the sheet for your eyes myself."

"But everybody else was a ghost, too," said Robert. "So I got a yellow piece of construction paper when I got to school for the party. Mike helped me cut it into a circle and I stuck it on the sheet with a safety pin—like a yolk. And then I was a fried egg." He paused for a few seconds. "And everybody knows that fried eggs sizzle."

"Well, you just go up to your room and write Mrs. Snead a note saying you're sorry you upset her."

"I didn't upset her, Mom. She's just always looking for something to tattle about. She's an old fungus face, and I hope she rots."

It was the meanest thing Robert had ever said in front of his mother.

"To your room. Now. And you won't go outside until the letter's written."

"How'd she know it was me, anyhow?" Robert asked. "I had a sheet over my head. It could have been anybody."

"Nobody else around here says 'twick-o'-

tweat,' " his older sister Leslie yelled from the laundry room where she was ironing a shirt. She was in the seventh grade and a junior varsity cheerleader. Everybody thought she was a big deal. Everybody except Robert.

"Too bad we're not all perfect—like you," he said to Leslie on his way up the stairs. He tried to make his r's come out right when he said it.

Robert fumbled in his drawer until he found an almost-clean piece of paper and a pencil. On the paper he wrote:

Dear Mrs. Snead,

I'm sorry if you thought I was hissing and spitting at you on Halloween. It was part of my costume as a fried egg. Thank you for the one piece of sugarless gum you gave out.

Sincerely,
Robert Reynolds

His cursive was shaky, and he couldn't remember if "spitting" had one *t* or two, but he thought the note was good enough to get him out of the house again.

Robert folded the paper twice, put it in his back pocket, and turned toward the window. He looked out at Mrs. Snead's house, and there, where nobody could see him, Robert Reynolds sizzled at her for five whole minutes.

Ashley Alston

Robert came down to dinner earlier than usual, put his note to Mrs. Snead where his mother would see it, and plopped down beside Leslie in the den to watch a rerun of "Little House on the Prairie." Robert liked to watch it in hopes of seeing snobby Nellie Oleson get taken down a peg or two. Nellie reminded him of Ashley Alston, who lived up the street. Robert and Ashley used to be friends, but lately things seemed different.

"Ashley Alston's father has to X-ray all her Halloween candy at the hospital before she can eat it," Robert said for no particular reason. Ashley's father was the town's only surgeon, and she was always talking about how important he was. "Isn't that the dumbest thing you've ever heard?" Robert asked Leslie.

"It's probably a good idea," said Leslie. She never seemed to agree with Robert about anything. "I feel sorry for Ashley," she went on, "up there in that big old house with nobody to play with. Her parents haven't let her out of their sight since she got bitten by that copperhead."

Robert recalled the incident well. He had been collecting rocks in a stream behind Ashley's house. "Your mother won't like it if you get your shoes wet," Robert had told her when Ashley asked if she could help him.

"I'll take my shoes off," said Ashley.

The running creek water had made each rock sparkle cold and shiny-smooth in their hands. Ashley had never collected rocks before. Robert figured he had one of the largest rock collections in all of Clarkston.

"I think this rock might be pure gold," Robert remembered yelling. When Ashley jumped from one rock to another to see Robert's find, a snake struck at her ankle. Ashley thought it felt like a bee sting, but Robert saw the snake's triangular head and the pits behind its eyes just before it slithered away. Robert made Ashley sit down on the bank with her leg lowered while he went to get her father. Robert had always expected girls to cry at the least thing, but she just sat there, stunned. Robert yelled all the way to her house. He had watched as Dr. Alston carried Ashley on his shoul-

der to the car and drove off toward the hospital, where she had stayed a few days.

After they had gone, Robert went to get the rocks he and Ashley had collected and put them in a little pile by her side door. The sun was beginning to dry them gray, and they didn't feel as cold or look as shiny anymore.

When she got back to class, Ashley showed everybody the two marks where the fangs had gone in and the big bruise on her arm where she got the antivenin shot that saved her life.

Her ankle was swollen and blue-black, like grape jelly on soft white bread. Only, jelly bread looked good. Ashley's ankle didn't.

Robert remembered feeling sorry for her when he saw the black-and-blue puffiness.

"Of course, I wouldn't have been bitten by the snake in the first place if Robert Reynolds hadn't made me look for rocks in that creek," Ashley announced to the circle of classmates gathered around her.

"Mostly, it was his fault," Ashley said. "Mother told me not to go near that creek, but Robert said it was safe. I should have known better."

That's it, Robert had thought. She's going to blame me.

"You think I'd jump around in a creek where I knew a snake was hiding?" Robert shouted. "You think I sicced that snake on you instead of me? You think I'm crazy or something?"

"That's enough," Miss McAfee, their teacher, had said. "I'm sure it was an accident, Robert.

We're all just glad Ashley's back with us so soon."

Robert's parents hadn't blamed him for the incident, and Dr. Alston had praised him for making Ashley sit calmly while he ran for help. "You kept a cool head," he had said.

Mrs. Alston told him she wanted Ashley to play with girls instead of boys for a while. So Robert had stayed away from her trampoline and her fish pond and her poodle named Pierre.

"Anybody want to help me set the table?" Mrs. Reynolds hollered from the kitchen. Her words jarred him away from snakes and back to dinner.

"Leslie would just love to," Robert said, mocking his mother's voice softly so she couldn't hear him.

Leslie clicked off the TV.

"But I want to see how it ends," Robert protested as his sister pulled his hair on her way to the dining room.

"It always ends the same," said Leslie. "Nellie Oleson always gets her own way."

"So do you," Robert shouted. "And so does Ashley Alston."

Leslie had already left the room.

Table Talk

When Robert sat down at the table, he noticed the avocados right away. The way Robert looked at it, God must have had a bad day when He invented avocados. Either that, or He had a sense of humor and liked to see the expression on people's faces when they bit into one for the first time.

Robert pretended to close his eyes while Judge Reynolds blessed the food. Robert liked his father's blessings best. They were shorter than his mother's.

"For this food, O Lord, we are thankful. Amen," he prayed.

I'm not thankful for these avocados, Robert thought. He had hidden three slices in his napkin before the blessing was finished. For once, he wished his mother was praying so that he'd have time to hide them all.

"So what happened at school?" Judge Reynolds asked as he passed the bread.

"Nothing much," said Robert. "Our hamster Rocky had babies."

"I take it Rocky was a girl," said Leslie.

"You're a mental giant," said Robert.

"At least I can say my r's."

"That's enough, Leslie," said Judge Reynolds. "Did anything unusual happen in your class today?"

"Well, I saw someone cheat on a spelling test," she said.

Robert took the remaining avocado slices out of his salad, mashed them with his fork, and dripped beef gravy over them.

"You know you have to eat everything on your plate," said Mrs. Reynolds. "No matter *what* you do to it."

"How did you handle that, Leslie?" Judge Reynolds wanted to know.

"Luckily, I didn't have to do anything, because the teacher saw him cheat, too. But I've been wondering all afternoon what I would've done if she hadn't seen it."

"Did you ever cheat on a test, Mom?" Robert asked.

"Not that I recall," said Mrs. Reynolds.

"Dad?"

"You have the makings of a lawyer in you, Robert Reynolds," said his father, laughing. "You always ask what's on your mind. That's good."

"And you"—Robert pointed his finger at his father and accused in his best courtroom style—"just changed the subject."

"I cheated once that I can remember," his father said. Robert knew he'd have to ask more questions to find out what happened. His father seldom answered more than he was asked.

"How old were you?"

"Seven. Maybe eight. Third grade, I think."

"What happened?"

"Didn't know if *i* came before *e* in 'received' or the other way around. I looked on Mildred Michaels's spelling test to find out. The teacher saw me."

"And what happened then?"

"The teacher tore up my paper and called my mother."

"And what happened then?"

"The worst punishment known to mankind."

"What did Grandma do to you? What did she do?"

Judge Reynolds smiled. "She made me eat avocados for supper for a whole week."

Leslie laughed. So did Robert. Mrs. Reynolds laughed a little, too.

"What did she *really* do?" Robert asked.

"She gave me a good lecture. Told me I was a Reynolds, and that I had to live up to my name. She said people forgive a misspelled word every now and then, but they never forget a cheater and they never forget a lie."

Robert felt a slice of his avocado fall from his

napkin onto their new rug. He hoped he could scrape it up with his foot before his mother noticed.

"Anybody ever lie to you in court?" Leslie asked.

"Sometimes they do," said Judge Reynolds. "It's called perjury. It's a whole separate crime to lie in court. Lying always makes things worse."

Robert's foot slipped and mashed the avocado into the rug. He bet God was laughing now.

"So who won the prize for the best costume at the Halloween party at school last night?" Mrs. Reynolds asked.

"Ashley Alston," Leslie said. "She went dressed as Little Bopeep. Had her dog dressed as a sheep and everything. Cutest costume you've ever seen."

"Only, sheep don't bark," said Robert. "That dumb poodle barked all night long. Little Bopeep and her barking sheep!"

"Robert," said Leslie, "if I didn't know better, I'd say you were jealous."

"Just because you like her doesn't mean I have to," said Robert.

"And just because you don't like avocados doesn't mean you can get away with hiding them in your napkin," Leslie stated proudly.

His parents both looked straight at him. They were not smiling.

Robert couldn't help but notice Leslie's grin.

Avocados and Ashley Alston, thought Robert as he felt the gravy-coated avocado slither down his throat a few seconds later. God must have a great sense of humor.

A Lesson in Manners

Robert's favorite part of fourth grade—if you didn't count lunch and recess—was show-and-tell. He loved it when he found a new rock to share, but he hadn't found any good ones for a week or so.

Right after Miss McAfee had taken roll, she asked if anyone had brought something to share with the class that day. Five hands wiggled in the air.

Chunkie Matthews went first. He brought a gerbil that wet on Miss McAfee's sweater. Chunkie scrunched up his face and flapped his arms when he realized what had happened. The class laughed. Miss McAfee laughed, too.

Pamela Gilbert brought a pomegranate she had gotten from a fancy grocery store in Richmond.

Nobody in Clarkston ate fancy fruit—just apples and oranges and such. She passed around a plate with a piece of pomegranate for everyone in the class. Robert didn't like the way the seeds stuck in his teeth when he tried to spit them at Mike while Miss McAfee wasn't looking.

Lee McCoy brought an arrowhead he had found with his father on a camping trip near Knoxville, Tennessee. It was sharp.

David Franklin brought a picture of the principal when she was a teenager. She was wearing a swimsuit, and her hair was tucked under a white swim cap. The bathing suit was tight, and the swim cap made her look bald. His grandmother had shown him the picture in her scrapbook.

"I borrowed it from my grandmother," David volunteered when Miss McAfee scowled at him.

"Did your grandmother know what you were going to do with that picture?" Miss McAfee asked.

"Not exactly," said David.

"Not at all," said Miss McAfee, as she sent David and his picture to go see the principal.

Then it was Ashley's turn for show-and-tell. She had carried her stuff to school in a canvas bookbag monogrammed *ABA* like everything else Ashley had. The *B* stood for brat, Robert had once suggested to his sister. Leslie said it stood for Beale. The name Beale was a very big deal in Clarkston, though Robert didn't exactly understand why.

Ashley wouldn't let anybody look into her monogrammed bag before show-and-tell, except Ceci Brackston and Joanie Crews, whom Ashley

ABA

had crowned her best friends of the week. When they looked, they *oohed*. And then they *ahhed*. And then they whispered. And then they giggled. Girls were like that, Robert decided.

Ashley brought her bag to the front of the room. She pulled a pink tablecloth out of it and spread it over an empty desk. Then she unwrapped a plate and a glass on a stem and a cloth napkin and some shiny silverware and placed them on top of the tablecloth. She finished the table setting with a fresh flower in a bud vase.

"Today, I'm going to show good manners," Ashley announced to the class cheerfully.

She sat down and pulled her chair close to the table.

"The first thing to do is to unfold the napkin across your lap. Never tuck it in your shirt."

This is the dumbest thing I've ever seen, thought Robert. He could tell from his classmates' faces that they agreed.

"Never drink water with food in your mouth," she went on. "And pay close attention to the way you use your knife and fork. Never cut up more than one piece of meat at a time. And *never ever* bite into a whole piece of bread. Remember the four B's: break bread before buttering," she said.

"If you do happen to get something on your mouth, remember to pat it gently with your napkin. This is the proper way to do it." Ashley demonstrated.

"And that's all the good manners I'm going to show you today," she said.

The class clapped softly, and Ashley gave Miss McAfee the rose.

"Thank you, Ashley," said Miss McAfee. "Your demonstration will be helpful to all of us, I'm sure." She paused, then said, "Now if no one else has anything to share, we'll go on to our multiplication problems." She turned and wrote on the blackboard. The class groaned.

Robert waited until lunch for his show-and-tell. The cafeteria was thick with the smell of kale and cornbread. Robert had brought his lunch, and he put his napkin carefully across his lap. He was sitting with Mike and David and Ian. Chunkie was sitting by himself at the end of the table. "I'm going to show you bad manners," he said, imitating Ashley's tone of voice. The people near him giggled, all except for Ceci and Joanie and Ashley. They were sitting at a table to the left, and they could hear, but they didn't laugh.

"First, you lick your knife, like this," he said, reaching for Mike's knife. He picked it up and licked the blade clean.

His friends began to laugh.

"Next, you never blow your nose on the napkin. You use your shirttail, like this." Robert buried his nose in his shirttail and snorted like a pig. His friends snorted, too. Robert noticed that Ashley had blushed to the color of her red corduroy jumper. She made a face at him.

"And most important of all," said Robert, "always chew with your mouth open—like this." He stuffed a candy bar from his lunch bag into his mouth, chewed it for a few seconds, and opened his mouth to show the gooey caramel and peanut bits. His friends laughed even louder.

Ashley took her tray back to the cafeteria kitchen before walking over to where Robert was still sitting.

"I really enjoyed your bad manners," Ashley said to Robert.

"Thank you, Ashley," Robert said gallantly.

"You know what I enjoyed most about it?" asked Ashley. Robert didn't answer her question, but she continued anyway.

"I wanted to see what the inside of your mouth looked like," she said. "I always wondered what there was about it that made your words come out funny." Ashley looked back at the table for Ceci and Joanie to join in her laughter, but neither one did.

Robert could feel his face flush with embarrassment. He stood up and looked straight into Ashley's eyes. Then he picked up his peanut-butter-and-jelly sandwich and smashed it in her face.

"Now, what is the proper way to remove *that* from your face?" Robert asked as Ashley wiped strawberry jelly from her eyelid.

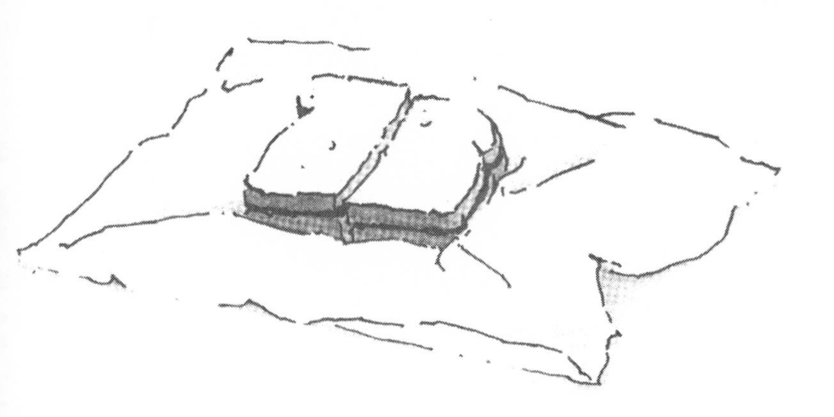

In Trouble

Robert sat inside the school office, replaying every line of their conversation in his mind. Miss McAfee had helped Ashley wash up in the rest room. She had told Robert to call his mother and ask her to come to school.

The secretary in the office had let him use the phone. Robert dialed his home number slowly, made a mistake, and dialed again. His mother picked up the phone on the second ring.

"Mom, Miss McAfee wants you to come to school to talk to her," Robert began.

"What happened, Robert?" Her voice was serious.

"I threw something at Ashley Alston."

"Did you hurt her? Was it a ball? A pencil? What happened? Is she all right?"

"A peanut-butter-and-jelly sandwich."

"Was it a joke?"

"I was mad at her."

"Well, young man, consider yourself in trouble."

Miss McAfee came into the office as Robert was hanging up.

"Mom'll be here in a few minutes," he said.

Robert sat down to wait for his mother. Through the window, he saw her station wagon pull up out front. Robert hadn't been able to tell Miss McAfee what had provoked his outburst. He was too ashamed to tell her.

Miss McAfee walked down the hall and waited on the front steps as Mrs. Reynolds got out of the car. They talked for a while before heading into school. Robert could hear them as they came through the office door.

"I can't imagine what got into Robert," his teacher said. "He's full of mischief, but there's not really a mean bone in his body."

"I'll get to the bottom of it when I get him home," his mother said.

"We'll see you tomorrow, Robert," Miss McAfee said. She didn't act angry. She even got Robert's jacket from the coat tree and handed it to him. Robert waved to his teacher as he left the office with his mother close behind.

Robert slid into the back seat of the car. His mother made him get out and sit up front.

He knew what his mother would say before she even said it.

"I've had it up to here with your behavior, Robert." She pointed to her neck. She always started out like that.

"I'm sick and tired of having Miss McAfee and Mrs. Snead and God knows who else upset by your actions." Sick and tired. The two words always went together when his mother said them.

"We'll just see what your father has to say about this." Robert knew his father usually didn't have as much to say as his mother did. He spent his whole day hearing about real crimes and punishing real criminals. By comparison, an assault with a peanut-butter-and-jelly sandwich might not seem so bad.

His mom wasn't yelling, but Robert could tell she wasn't happy with him. Robert stared out the window.

"Look at me when I talk to you, Robert," she said.

Robert kept on staring out the window.

"You better look at me, young man."

Robert turned around. Tears were brewing in his eyes. He expected her to ask if he wanted her to give him something to cry about. This time, she didn't say it.

"What's wrong, Robert?" Her voice wasn't as stern now.

"I don't care if everyone in Clarkston makes fun of the way I talk," he yelled. They had pulled into the driveway of their house. Tears were streaming down his cheeks.

"And you can tell that Ashley Alston I said so," he said, as he slammed the door and ran to his room.

Robert sprawled out across his bed and began to shuffle his baseball cards, then lined them up in order of batting averages. Usually, when Robert was in big trouble, he would wait in his room until his father knocked on the door. He had a long time to wait since school wasn't even over yet, and his father didn't get home until six.

This time, though, his mother's knock came first. She was standing in the hall with a glass of milk and a ham sandwich on whole-wheat bread toasted light brown.

"I thought you might like some lunch since I take it you didn't finish yours." She was smiling. "I thought about fixing you peanut butter and jelly, but I was afraid you might throw it at me." Robert knew that was her idea of a joke. It wasn't really funny, but at least she was trying.

"You want to tell me what Ashley said that hurt your feelings?"

"She made fun of the way I say my r's."

"I think I know how you felt," said Mrs. Reynolds. "When I was about your age, I was chubby, and there was a boy on the block who always yelled, 'Fatty, fatty, two by four, couldn't get through the bathroom door, so she did it on the floor.' " Robert couldn't imagine his mother being fat. She was skinny now. His mother laughed at the memory.

"How come you're laughing about it?" Robert asked. "Doesn't sound that funny to me."

"Oh, I didn't think it was funny then. I wish I had thought to throw a peanut-butter-and-jelly sandwich at him."

His mother's voice was soft.

"There are worse things in life than not saying your r's right," she said.

Robert picked the ham out of the sandwich and left the bread on his plate.

"Why don't you let me sign you up for speech classes, Robert? Your father and I have talked about it often, but we thought it would be better if you made the decision to go yourself. There's really nothing to be embarrassed about."

Robert knew what his mother said was true, but he still didn't like the idea of going. It wasn't so much the lessons he dreaded. He just didn't want anyone to know that his problem was so big he needed help.

He started shuffling his baseball cards again.

"Do you want people to make fun of your speech for the rest of your life, or do you want to do something about it?"

"OK, Mom, I'll go," Robert said.

"I'll try to get an appointment for tomorrow, before you chicken out," said his mother.

"You don't have to worry about me chickening out."

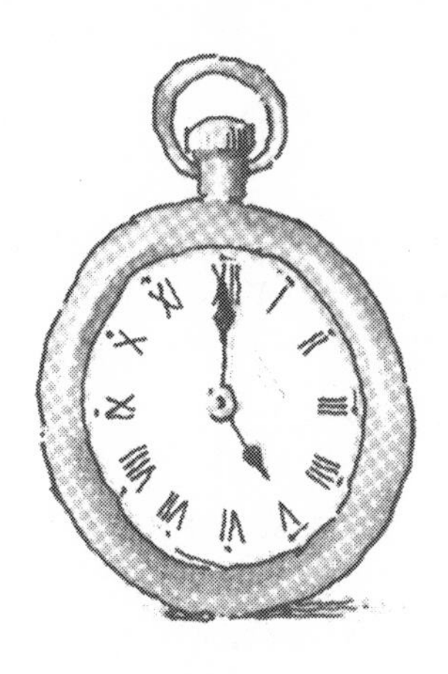

The Verdict

Judge Reynolds came home at five instead of six and suggested they take a long walk. Robert knew his mother had already told him about what had happened. His father always suggested a long walk when they had something important to talk about.

"You want to tell me about it?" Judge Reynolds began.

Robert told him about Ashley's good manners and his bad manners and her comment about his r's and how she looked with peanut butter up her nose.

Robert thought he heard his father chuckle, but Judge Reynolds's face was serious when Robert glanced at him out of the corner of his eye.

They walked—the two of them—past the post

office and by the courthouse. Two men on a bench tipped their hats and said, "Good evenin' Judge," to Robert's father. Judge Reynolds nodded back.

"A person can't help how he feels," Judge Reynolds said at last. "Feelings aren't right or wrong." He paused to let his words sink in. "It's how you react to your feelings that makes the difference."

"I didn't react very well, I guess," said Robert.

"No, you didn't, Robert, but it's understandable in a way. Not right, but understandable. The law talks a lot about premeditation."

Robert knew he was about to get a lecture on the law again. It was one of his father's favorite things to talk about.

"Premeditation means you intend to do what you do . . . you know it's wrong, but you do it anyway. If something is premeditated, the punishment is always worse."

Robert thought he understood.

"What you did was still wrong," said Judge Reynolds.

"What about what Ashley said?" Robert wanted her to take part of the blame, too. Just like she had blamed him for being bitten by the copperhead.

"You should have walked away from her, Robert. Either that, or had the courage to tell her how you felt when she said it."

Robert couldn't even imagine admitting to Ashley that she had hurt his feelings.

"Are you ashamed of me?" Robert asked.

"I'll never be ashamed of *you*," said Judge Reynolds. "I may be ashamed of something you

do, but I'll never be ashamed of you. There's a difference."

Robert noticed they were walking toward Ashley's house.

"How would you feel about talking to Ashley about what happened?" Judge Reynolds asked.

"You think I ought to, don't you?"

"That's entirely up to you, Robert. But if you think you should, I'll be happy to go with you for moral support."

Dr. Alston answered the door. When Robert said he had come to apologize to Ashley, Dr. Alston invited them into the house. The carpet was thick. There was a statue in the entrance hall, and it was naked.

Dr. Alston said Ashley was resting. She hadn't felt well all afternoon.

"I'm sorry this happened, Jake," Judge Reynolds said.

"It'll give the town something to talk about for a while," Dr. Alston said. He wasn't uppity like Ashley. Robert thought Mrs. Alston was nice, too, even if she had blamed him for the snakebite. He didn't know what had happened to Ashley. One day she seemed to like him; the next day, she didn't. Robert just couldn't figure girls out at all.

"Don't worry about it," Dr. Alston said to Robert. "I'm sure you two will be able to work it out. Besides, I've been in a scuffle or two myself—only we usually fought with rocks or water guns, not peanut-butter sandwiches."

"I can remember those days," said Judge Reynolds. Both men laughed and shook hands. It occurred to Robert that Dr. Alston's hands were bigger than his father's.

"I've been noticing lately that grownups laugh about bad things they did when they were kids," Robert said as they left the Alstons' yard.

"Time has a way of making things better," said Judge Reynolds.

"Does it make everything better?" Robert wanted to know.

"Everything I've ever known," said Judge Reynolds. "Except maybe your mother's broccoli casserole. It never gets any better. Don't tell her I said so, though."

"Do you think my speech will get better in time?" asked Robert.

"I'm sure of it, Robert. You're taking a big step tomorrow, aren't you? Your mom told me you wanted her to make an appointment for you at the speech clinic. I'm proud of you."

Robert thought about telling his father that he actually hadn't been thrilled about her making the appointment, but he didn't.

Instead, Robert got up the courage to ask his father something he had been wondering.

"Do you remember when Leslie was bawling because someone gave her doll a buzz cut, and I blamed it on my G.I. Joe?"

Judge Reynolds remembered.

"And you said if G.I. Joe did such a thing, he needed to be put in jail at the top of your closet for at least a month."

Judge Reynolds laughed.

"I hated not being able to play with him."

Judge Reynolds laughed again. So did Robert.

"You knew all along that I did it, didn't you?"

"You'd be surprised at what I know," said Judge Reynolds.

Then he said it again, this time a little softer. "You'd be surprised at what I know."

Macon Cooper

"Did you get in trouble?" Mike wanted to know, as he and Robert were throwing papers the next morning. They shared a paper route that extended from Main Street to the junction—almost two miles. Every morning, eighty-eight families in Clarkston woke up to the *Daily News* that the two friends had chauffeured to them on their ten-speed bikes.

"They were just disappointed," Robert said. "I hate that the worst."

"But wasn't it worth it to see the look on Ashley's face?" Mike asked. He always could find the best side of a situation.

"Do people talk about the way I say my r's a lot?" Robert asked.

"Maybe once in a while," Mike said.

"Remember when we phoned old Mrs. Snead and asked if her refrigerator was running, and she said yes, and we told her she'd better go catch it?" The two laughed. Making prank phone calls had been their favorite thing to do when they were seven. "And I got caught because she said nobody else pronounced 'refrigerator' and 'running' like I did?"

"Don't let it bother you, Robert," Mike said. "I got caught, too, and I *can* say my r's right."

"It didn't help that my sister picked up the other phone just when we got to the best part," Robert said. "Good old Leslie. Never did anything wrong in her whole life." The two pedaled as fast as they could past Mrs. Snead's house. They didn't have to stop there anymore. She had quit taking the paper last month.

"Can we meet at the tree house after school?" Mike asked as Robert turned into his driveway.

"Gotta go somewhere," Robert yelled back.

"Where?" Mike asked. "You taking piano lessons or something?"

"I got a secret mission," Robert shot back. "Can't tell anybody about it yet."

"I bet it's piano lessons," Mike countered, as he scattered gravel on his way down the street.

"What's this about a secret mission?" his mother asked as Robert almost slammed the door behind him. She was breaking eggs into a bowl. Robert hoped she scrambled them hard today. He hated runny eggs. "You haven't forgotten about your appointment with Miss Cooper, have you?"

"I haven't forgotten," Robert said. "I'll ride my bike to her office."

"Well, I better see it there if I drive by," said his mother.

"I don't want to park my bike out front, Mom. You think I want everybody to know I'm going there?"

"There is nothing wrong with getting help," his father said calmly. "It's nothing to be embarrassed about, son."

"I hate it when my eggs are runny," Robert said, careful to pronounce "runny" as best he could. He was anxious to change the subject. "I think I'll just eat cereal."

Robert didn't know what to expect when he parked his bike in back of the speech clinic and knocked on the door.

MACON COOPER—SPEECH THERAPIST, the sign on the front of the office said. A woman came to the front door and shook hands with Robert. Her skin was soft, and she smelled like flowers. "I'm Macon Cooper," she said. "Your mother has told me a lot about you."

"I've never known anyone named Macon before," Robert said. "It's a pretty name, though. I like it." She motioned him into her office.

"I used to want to be named something else," Miss Cooper said. "Like Mary or Karen or Julie."

She laughed when she said it. "People used to make fun of my name. They called me Macon A. Mess, or they'd say, 'Macon, Macon, smells like bacon.' "

"Do you like your name?" she asked Robert.

"Not so much, really," Robert said.

"Why not?"

" 'Cause the first day of school the new teacher always asks what my name is and I can't say my r's, so I say, 'It's Wobet Weynolds,' and everybody laughs. It always happens that way."

"Well, it looks to me like we've got two choices," Miss Cooper said. She wore a gold chain around her neck, and every few minutes she would twist it around her fingers.

"You can change your name to something you *can* say—like Otis or Nathan or Lionel or Melvin or Elmo. Or . . ." She paused to make her point. Her nails were smooth, with white tips showing through pale polish.

"Or you could learn to say 'Robert' correctly." She paused again.

"Will it be Elmo? Or Robert?" she then asked.

"Wobet."

"Let's try that again."

Miss Cooper showed Robert in a mirror how to make his tongue do *r* sounds. Then Robert listened to tapes and tried to say the *r* words better. Miss Cooper told him when he said the words correctly and when he needed to try again.

Then she showed him pictures of words that begin with *r* and made Robert say them. Robert liked some of the things she made him pronounce, like Reebok tennis shoes and Redskin football players and race cars and root beer and raisins. When she showed him a picture of a rattlesnake, Robert told her how much he hated snakes. After what had happened to Ashley, he would never like snakes again.

"We'll get this problem solved a lot quicker if you'll practice these drills every night," said Miss Cooper. She gave him some records and a workbook to practice with.

Then she handed Robert a rock he had been admiring on her desk. She said she had gotten it out West. It was the shiniest rock Robert had ever seen.

"When you can say 'rock' correctly, it's yours to keep," Miss Cooper said. "Until then, you can borrow it for good luck."

Robert put the rock in his pocket.

"Now, remember, I'm going to call you Elmo until you tell me how to pronounce your real name," Miss Cooper said when he got ready to leave. She held his baseball jacket for him as he punched his arms into the sleeves.

"Elmo? Do you have to call me Elmo?"

"Don't worry," Miss Cooper said. "A lot of my favorite people are named Elmo."

The TADs

"Robert says meet him at the tree house Saturday at noon," Mike told Ian, who told David, who promised not to tell anyone else.

The next day, the boys climbed the rungs to the tree house, all except for Mike, who shinnied up the other side of the trunk to save time.

Inside, they sat still, listening to Robert's plans. On that day, Robert's tree house became the TADs' clubhouse. Since it was *his* tree house, Robert got to make up the rules.

Rule number 1. An official TAD could never tell what the letters stood for. *T* stood for Take. *A* stood for A. *D* stood for Dare. Take a Dare.

Rule number 2. An official TAD could never tell

how someone got initiated into the club . . . that he had to take one of the most awful dares ever thought of in Clarkston.

Rule number 3. An official TAD could never tell the secret handshake (two short squeezes), the official knock (two short knocks), or the official whistle (two short whistles).

Rule number 4. An official TAD could never tell anyone else what the inside of the clubhouse looked like. On the outside, everyone could see that it was painted white to match the Reynolds house, but on the inside, it would be a different story. After initiation, each TAD would paint a part of the wall any way he wanted to.

Mike wanted to paint the door with lightning bolts. Ian wanted to paint the ceiling like clouds. David wanted to paint one whole wall with his footprints. Robert wanted to paint his wall to look like a big bull's-eye, and he wanted to put Ashley Alston's picture right in the middle.

But before the painting came the dares. Everyone who wanted to be a TAD had to write a really funny dare on a slip of paper, drop it into a coffee can, and pick out someone else's slip with his eyes closed. If he got his own, he had to put it back. Mike picked first.

"Push Mrs. Snead's doorbell for ten seconds and run away without getting caught," he read. That wasn't too bad, Robert thought. He had done that lots of times.

David went next. "Hoist a pair of girls' underwear up the school flagpole before the safety patrol raises the flag next Monday." Everyone laughed. Robert thought that would be harder.

"Burp three times—really loud—over the take-out loudspeaker at Harold's Hamburger Haven," Ian read.

"You're gonna get caught," Mike predicted. "And Harold's real mean."

Then it was Robert's turn. He picked the last piece of paper out of the coffee can. He read it twice before he could believe what he had to do. It was the worst possible dare he could imagine. "Go on a hike up Cattail Creek Falls with Chunkie Matthews—and take a picture of you and Chunkie at the top."

Robert had never known anybody like Chunkie Matthews. Chunkie's real name was Chuckie, but nobody ever called him that. Chunkie had been different ever since the first time Robert had met him in kindergarten. When the other kids were cutting out pictures with plastic scissors, Chunkie had sat in the corner and eaten the white paste. With his stomach protruding like a beach ball over his skinny belt, Chunkie was just plain chunky. He kind of looked like a chipmunk. When he got really excited, Chunkie flapped his arms. Robert could just imagine Chunkie's chipmunk face flushed red with excitement when Robert called him after the club meeting.

But all Chunkie said was, "You mean you want *me* to go hiking with *you*?"

. . .

They met at the NO TRESPASSING sign after church the next day. Of all the dumb dares, Robert thought, watching Chunkie bat gnats as they wound their way up Cattail Creek. Chunkie took two little hopping steps for every one Robert took. He stopped at every bend to make sure his shoelaces were tied.

"I can't go any farther," he moaned about halfway up. "I'm exhausted. Honest, I am."

"The falls are just around the bend," Robert said, handing him a walking stick. "There's trout as big around as your arms swimming up there."

Chunkie winced. Robert wished he hadn't said that part about his arms.

"Let's sing," Robert said. "It makes the walk go faster."

"There was an old man named Michael Finnegan." Robert began an old folk song he had learned from his father when they had gone hiking a few years before. He had forgotten the exact words, so he made them up as he went along. *"He grew whiskers on his chinnegan."* Robert marched in time to the music. Chunkie tried to march, too. He tripped over a branch. *"A man pulled 'em out, but they grew in again."* Chunkie was laughing now, beating time with his walking stick. *"Poor old Michael Finnegan. Begin again."*

The last hundred yards, Robert had to pull Chunkie along by the forearm. Then they were there at the top, catching their breath, watching the trout frolic. Chunkie ate a candy bar and stuffed the wrapper in his back pocket.

"They really are as big as my arms," he said after a while.

"Your arms aren't so big," Robert said.

"Sure they are," said Chunkie. "So's the rest of me. That's why they call me Chunkie."

Robert couldn't think of anything to say.

"I wish I weren't so fat," Chunkie said. Robert couldn't imagine Chunkie thin. Thinner, maybe. But not thin.

"You made it to the top, Chunkie," Robert said, changing the subject.

"You won't tell anybody that I mind being fat, will you, Robert?" Chunkie pleaded, as if he suddenly regretted telling his biggest secret.

"I won't tell."

Robert wanted to tell him about his r's and about Miss Cooper and about his secret trip to the speech clinic. Instead, he took his arm and pulled Chunkie to his feet.

"Hey, let's take some pictures," Robert said, feeling a little guilty about the suggestion. He took a picture of Chunkie leaning on his walking stick. Then Chunkie took one of Robert skipping rocks. Robert couldn't figure out how to take a picture of them together.

"Maybe you could hold it out as far as you can reach and take a close-up of us," Chunkie suggested. Robert stretched the camera as far as he could and clicked the shutter while he and Chunkie made funny faces.

"I'd like to buy one from you if they turn out good," said Chunkie.

"I'll give you one," said Robert. "You don't have to pay me."

"This is the most fun I've ever had in my whole life," said Chunkie.

"We'd better be going, Chuckie," Robert said. "You don't mind if I call you Chuckie from now on, do you?"

The Monsters

Robert heard Leslie practicing the piano when he got home. "*Come, we thankful people, come,*" she sang as she picked out the tune.

Robert smashed two black keys at the end of the piano as he passed.

"Will you please stop it!" Leslie yelled. "In case you haven't noticed, I am *practicing*. I am playing in front of the *whole church* on Thanksgiving."

"Which is *truly* something for us *all* to be thankful for," Robert said as he pounded the keys once more.

"As long as you're both at the piano, Leslie, why don't you play your brother's song?" their mother suggested from the kitchen. Miss Cooper had said that sometimes it's easier to sing r's correctly than to say them.

"I might as well," Leslie said. "I've got a while to practice before Thanksgiving." Robert slid onto the piano bench beside her.

"I've been working on the railroad," Leslie began singing, as she played the tune with her right hand and added a chord or two with her left. She really does play well, Robert thought, but he didn't say it.

Leslie started over. This time, Robert sang with her. He tried hard to remember how Miss Cooper said to hold his tongue when the "railroad" word came around. He wondered how his words sounded to Leslie.

"How were my r's?" Robert asked when they finished the song.

"Better than your *singing*," Leslie said.

"I hate practicing my drills," said Robert.

"Nobody likes to practice anything," said Leslie. "I myself hate practicing the piano, but I like the way it feels when I finally get it right."

Robert thought about Chuckie. He wondered if Chuckie somehow could practice to make people like him better—or at least tease him less.

"I like the way you play," Robert said softly.

After dinner, Robert's mother helped him do his r drills. She showed him the flash cards he was supposed to pronounce and made him say the words correctly over and over. Robert thought he was getting better, but he couldn't be sure.

Robert didn't sleep well the night before his sec-

ond visit to the speech clinic. He sprawled on his back and thought about what would happen the next day. He saw himself going into the speech clinic. He could see Miss Cooper saying, "Let me see, I believe your name is Elmo."

Robert pictured himself saying, "No. You are wrong. My name is Robert. Robert Reynolds." His r's would be perfect, and Miss Cooper would hug him to her. She would smell like his mother's cold cream, only better.

Instead, Robert went back to the clinic after school, careful not to let anyone see him get out of his mother's car. He practiced his drills over and over with Miss Cooper. Even though Robert didn't say his r's perfectly, Miss Cooper made him feel good. "You're close," she said. "I can see that rock's going to be yours to keep." Robert had been carrying the rock with him almost everywhere he went. He knew now it wouldn't make him say his r's better, but it made him feel good to have it in his pocket.

When his mother picked him up from the clinic, Robert asked her what "You're close" really meant. They had stopped for a double cheeseburger and large fries at Harold's Hamburger Haven on the way home.

"Does 'You're close' mean the same thing as 'You're wrong'?"

"Never thought of it that way," Mrs. Reynolds said. "Come to think of it, I guess it can mean that. It's all in the way a person looks at it."

"Miss Cooper makes me feel close," said Robert. "Ashley Alston makes me feel wrong."

"Are you still fretting over what Ashley said to you?"

"Not so much anymore," Robert said. Robert knew his mother knew he wasn't telling the truth.

"I think what we need is a big can of Ashley Alston spray," said Mrs. Reynolds.

Robert laughed. He hadn't thought of his father's sprays in a long time.

"Remember the wolf spray your father used to squirt under your bed at night when you were afraid wolves might be hiding under there?"

"Aw, Mom," said Robert. "I was real little then."

"And the monster spray, too. Don't forget the monster spray he squirted in the closet."

Robert remembered making his father come into his room every night to protect him from wolves and monsters before he went to sleep. He didn't know at the time that wolf spray and monster spray were just cans of his mother's hair spray with the labels torn off.

"I know there never really was a monster in the closet," said Robert. He was grinning.

"The monsters we're afraid of *aren't* there most of the time," Mrs. Reynolds said.

Robert wasn't exactly sure what his mother meant, but, like Macon Cooper, she made him feel close.

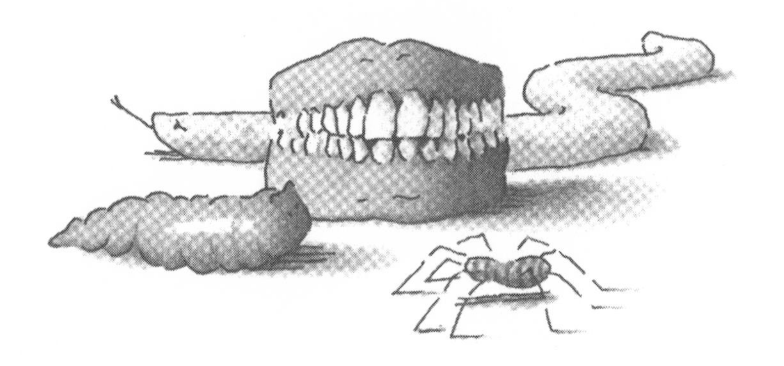

Confessions

The next Saturday just before noon the TADs met at the tree house to report on their dares. Mike bragged that he had pushed Mrs. Snead's doorbell for ten seconds. Robert had witnessed the whole thing from his porch.

Ian Taylor had ordered four hamburgers, five orders of fries, and six drinks before he belched three times into the loudspeaker at Harold's. "He did it really loud," said David Franklin, who had gone inside to order a vanilla cone.

Both Robert and Mike had seen a pair of girls' underwear flying half-mast from the flagpole on their morning paper route. "Way to go, David," Robert had yelled, as they passed by the school.

"I could have been in big trouble," David confessed. "It was my sister's underwear, and I almost forgot to rip out the nametag Mom sewed in when my sister went to camp." The other TADs snickered.

"Were you scared you'd get caught?" Ian asked David.

"I don't scare easily," boasted David. "I can't think of anything I'm really scared of anymore."

"Everybody's scared of something," said Ian. "For me, it's spiders. I have hated them my whole life."

"Eensy-weensy spider went up the waterspout," Mike began singing in his worst voice. *"Down came the rain and washed the spider out."* By now, the others were singing, too, but the song had turned to shrieks. *"Out came the sun and dried up all the rain."* Ian tried to make a spider shadow on the wall of the tree house, but it was too dark. *"And the eensy-weensy spider went up the spout again."*

"You'll never believe what I used to be scared of," Mike said.

"Taking a bath?" asked David. "Is that why you used to stink?"

"Very funny, David," said Mike. "You're a real comedian. For your information, I was afraid of slugs."

"Slugs?" all three boys said at the same time. Then they laughed.

"Slimy old slugs," said Mike. He was laughing, too. "I was so afraid of stepping on a slug that I slept with my shoes on."

"Slept with your shoes on?" Robert gasped. "Why did you do that?"

"So in case our house caught on fire in the middle of the night and we didn't have time to dress before we ran out, I wouldn't step on a slug barefooted."

"That's about the stupidest thing I've ever heard," said Ian.

"Which is why I've never told anyone before," said Mike. "I knew you guys would tease me. Slugs seemed so scary to me at the time, though."

"Now that I think about it, there was one thing that really scared me when I was little," confessed David at last. "False teeth!"

"False teeth?"

"Yeah. We used to have this white-haired baby-sitter, and when we gave her a hard time, she'd take out her false teeth and snap them at us. I couldn't figure out how hers came out and mine didn't. Those false teeth really gave me the creeps. She was our best baby-sitter, though," David said. "She made us popcorn balls when we were good, which wasn't all that often. She couldn't even eat popcorn because of her false teeth. What are you afraid of, Robert?" asked David, anxious to change the subject.

Robert thought about telling them he was always afraid that people would tease him about the way he said his r's. He thought about it, but he didn't admit it because he was sure his friends would torment him, the way they did with Chuckie. Then he considered telling them about the monster sprays his father had invented. Instead, he said he was scared of snakes. It was safe to be afraid of snakes, he reasoned.

"Did you see any snakes on your hike with good old Chunkie?" asked Ian.

"That's right. Where's the picture of you and Chunkie?" David chimed in.

From his hip pocket, Robert took a colored print of two out-of-focus faces with mountains in the background. "Yep, it's Chunkie all right," said David. "I can tell from his chipmunk cheeks."

"We'll put it in the bull's-eye when you paint it," said Ian, grabbing the picture from David. "Robert and Ashley and Chunkie, all three right there together."

"Give it back," yelled Robert. "That wasn't part of the dare." Ian threw the picture to David, who put it in his mouth. The others laughed so hard that Robert was afraid his mother would hear and wonder what they were up to.

"Chuckie's not all that bad," Robert said, but the others were laughing too loud to hear him.

A Matter of Honor

"If your grades don't get better, we'll have to close the tree house for a while," Robert's father said when he saw Robert's report card a few days later. "You've been spending a lot of time up there."

Robert knew his father always meant what he said.

"I really need to make a good grade in geography," he admitted to Leslie before dinner that night. "I'm not doing so well in it this time."

Leslie had guessed as much. Miss McAfee was the hardest teacher she had ever had, too. Why, she herself had made her first B in that class. She usually got straight A's. As for Robert, his A's and B's were few and far between, and this time, he had even managed to get a D in penmanship.

After dinner, Leslie volunteered to help Robert learn the state capitals for his big test the next day. She made index cards with the state on one side and the capital on the other. They shuffled the cards and Robert drew them one by one, trying to say the capital without looking. He got a point for every one he could name; Leslie got a point for every one he couldn't. The loser had to be the winner's servant for a day.

"Tennessee," Leslie said.

"Nashville."

"Texas" was the second card he got.

"Dallas," Robert guessed. Leslie got that point.

"South Dakota" was the third.

"Pierre," Robert guessed correctly. "Like the name of Ashley's dog."

"Vermont."

"Montpewee." Robert gave it his best guess.

"Close, but not close enough," declared Leslie. "Montpelier is right, though. Miss McAfee won't count it right if it's not spelled correctly."

By bedtime, Robert knew the capitals of all fifty states backwards and forwards, east to west, north to south.

"Thanks, Leslie," he said, as his sister proclaimed him the winner and herself his servant for the next day. "You help me with my r's, and they're getting better. You help me with my geography. I

UGUSTA

hope it gets better, too. You'd make a great teacher." He realized that may have been the only nice thing he had said to Leslie all year. "I should be *your* servant tomorrow."

"A deal is a deal," said Leslie. "You won. I have to be your servant."

The next day, Robert couldn't wait for the test. He stroked Miss Cooper's rock in his pocket for good luck. It would be his to keep before too much longer, he hoped. If he kept on practicing, it would be his.

The test was a hard one. Thirty fill-in-the-blanks, ten matching, ten multiple choice. But Robert felt good about it. He might have forgotten one or two, but no more. I might have even gotten a hundred, he thought to himself.

Miss McAfee handed the tests back two days later. Instead of the one hundred he was expecting, Robert got a "See me after school" written in red ink at the top of his paper. Maybe Miss McAfee's going to congratulate me in person, he thought.

He noticed Ashley lingering after school, too.

Miss McAfee started off nice. About how the other grades on the test had been bad. About how both of them seemed to know the capitals almost perfectly.

"But there is one thing I'm curious about," she said. Her tone got serious.

"Isn't it a coincidence that you both missed the same two questions, and the answers you gave were identical, too. You both wrote that July was the capital of Maine, and Saint Mark was the capital of Minnesota. The correct answers were Augusta and Saint Paul."

"I knew that one of the months was the capital of Maine and one of the saints was the capital of Minnesota," said Robert. "I guessed the wrong ones, I suppose."

Robert didn't know what else to say. For a few seconds, it didn't occur to him that he was being accused of cheating.

"You did sit beside Ashley during the test, didn't you, Robert?" Miss McAfee asked.

Robert nodded yes.

"Did you see Robert looking on your paper, Ashley?" Miss McAfee asked.

"No," she said softly. "No, I didn't."

"Did you happen to glance at Ashley's answers accidentally?" she asked Robert.

"No, I did not," said Robert not so softly. He knew Miss McAfee would never believe that Ashley with her A+ average would even think of cheating. So she must have thought that he had looked at her answers.

"Leslie made me flash cards and we studied those capitals all night," Robert blurted out. "I knew them perfectly when I went to bed."

Ashley knew that he was telling the truth. She had heard him talking about how hard they had studied before the test began.

"I didn't cheat, Miss McAfee," Robert shouted. "I'd never cheat. My dad says that's the worst thing a person can do—cheat and lie—and I'd never do it 'cause I've got to live up to my name."

Miss McAfee saw tears at the bottom of Robert's eyes. He mopped them away with the sleeve of his shirt.

"Then it just must have been a coincidence, a very strange coincidence," Miss McAfee said deliberately. Robert could tell from her voice she still didn't believe him. Robert hated her at that moment.

"You may go now," she said. "I'll think about this some more over the weekend."

"I didn't cheat," shouted Robert. "I'm not going to leave until you believe me."

Robert noticed that Ashley had sat down in the chair beside the teacher's desk. She dangled her shoes on the rungs of the chair. Then she put her face in her hands and started to cry.

"Robert's right. He didn't cheat," Ashley said softly when Miss McAfee came close to comfort her.

"What do you mean?" Miss McAfee asked.

Ashley looked first at Robert, then at Miss McAfee.

"I didn't study the state capitals, but I knew Robert did. I knew you expected me to make a hundred and my parents expected me to make a hundred. I didn't want to let anyone down."

Ashley was crying so hard she couldn't catch her breath.

"So I looked on Robert's paper," she said, sobbing. "It's the worst thing I've done in my whole entire life."

Robert backed out of the room. He didn't want

to stay there and watch what was bound to happen next. It didn't take an A+ student to know that Ashley Alston was in very big trouble.

If she hadn't told the truth, Robert thought, Miss McAfee would never have believed me. Only she did. Ashley had cheated, but she didn't lie. She hadn't perjured herself.

Robert was glad Ashley wasn't guilty of that crime, too.

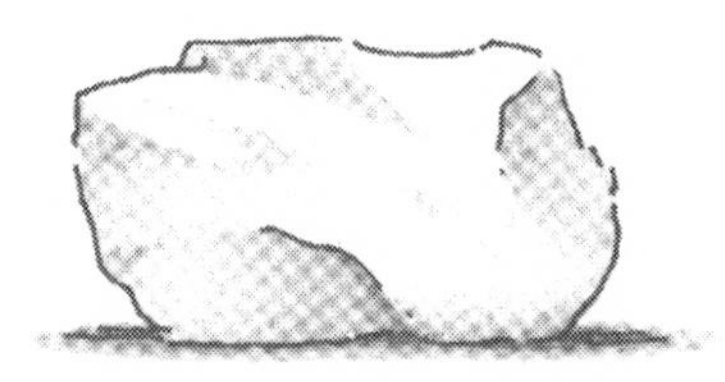

The Shiniest Rock of All

The same day Miss McAfee had accused Robert of cheating, his father answered the phone during dinner. Robert could tell from Judge Reynolds's face that he wasn't pleased at what he was hearing.

Robert poked at his beets, watching the red juice puddle in his plate. He heard Judge Reynolds tell the person on the phone that he'd see to it amends were made.

"Mrs. Snead says someone has ruined her best boxwood bush, the one in her side yard," Judge Reynolds began when he sat back down at the table. "She says it was a good one, and very expensive." Robert didn't look up.

"You wouldn't know anything about that bush, would you, Robert?" Judge Reynolds asked.

"Why's she always picking on me, anyway? She's the worst old fungus face in Clarkston." That was still Robert's favorite thing to say about Mrs. Snead.

"Did you ruin her bush? Yes or no?"

"I climbed her tree to get a ball that was stuck there, Dad," Robert said. "And a limb broke, and I fell out of the tree onto her dumb old bush. I know I should have told her, but she always makes such a big deal about everything." Robert paused. "How'd she know it was me, anyway?"

"Just a lucky guess," Leslie suggested.

"I've told you to stay away from her house," Judge Reynolds said. "If you hadn't been in her yard and in her tree, her bush would be just fine now, wouldn't it? You could have been hurt, you know," he added gently as an afterthought.

Robert knew his father was right. Even if it had been his best ball stuck up there in her tree. How was he to know the branch where he was climbing would go and break?

After supper, Robert and his father went to Mrs. Snead's house. Robert could tell she really wanted to yell at him, only she couldn't because his father was there. Mrs. Snead told Judge Reynolds he ought to give Robert a good whipping with a switch from one of the branches he'd been climbing on. Instead, Judge Reynolds made Robert buy a new boxwood bush with money he had earned on his paper route. Even worse, he made him plant it on Sunday afternoon—during the Redskins–Cowboys football game. Robert had wanted to watch that game on television more than anything.

Robert dug a hole and buried the roots of the new bush, then flooded the roots with a water hose and packed the dirt down tight. It was an unusually hot weekend in November. The sun scorched Robert's back and made his cotton shirt smell like ironing.

Robert had just finished patting the wet soil around the bush when he saw Ashley Alston riding by on her bike. He hadn't seen her since Friday when Miss McAfee had accused him of cheating. Robert ran to the road, not stopping to turn off the hose, not even stopping for the boxwood bush in Mrs. Snead's front yard.

Ashley dragged her foot to stop the bike. She didn't look up until Robert spoke.

"Hi, Ashley," Robert said.

"My parents got real upset with me," Ashley said as if answering Robert's unasked question.

"I've been known to upset my parents a time or two," said Robert. He was grinning. "As a matter of fact, I'm being punished right now."

He told Ashley about Mrs. Snead and the Redskins–Cowboys game he was missing and the paper route money he had to use to buy a new bush.

"But I did worse," said Ashley. "You said so yourself. You said cheating and lying are the worst things a person can do."

"You don't have to be perfect to be darned good," Robert said. It was a dumb thing to say, he thought. He wished he hadn't said it.

"I'm not gonna tell anyone, in case you're wondering," Robert went on. He wished he hadn't said that, either. "It'll be a secret."

A little while ago, Robert had wanted to put Ashley's picture right in the middle of the bull's-eye in his clubhouse. Now he felt downright sorry for her. Things were so confusing sometimes. I may be the only person in the world, thought Robert, who knows that Chuckie Matthews is better than everyone thinks—and Ashley Alston is worse.

Somehow, at this moment, Robert actually liked them both.

"You shouldn't hate yourself just because you made a mistake," Robert said softly.

"Why not?"

Robert thought a minute. " 'Cause it's not *good manners*."

It was another dumb thing to say, but it made Ashley laugh.

"That was a really mean thing I said," Ashley admitted. "I bet I looked funny with peanut butter on my face."

"And strawberry jelly on your eyelid," added Robert. They both laughed again.

"Want to know a secret about me?" Robert asked. "Something I've never told anyone before?"

"I guess so, if you want to tell me," said Ashley.

Robert found himself telling Ashley about his r's and about how Miss Cooper wouldn't have to call him Elmo much longer. It made him feel great that he didn't have to keep it a secret anymore. Then he told her all about Miss Cooper's rock—how it just sat there in his pocket and when he felt the worst, it made good things happen. He took the rock and showed it to Ashley, turning it over, tossing it in the air and catching it behind his back.

"You can borrow it for a while," he said. "It's not mine to give away just yet, but it might be soon. I'll let you know if I need it."

He watched as Ashley slid the rock into her hip pocket and pedaled down the street.

Mrs. Snead was standing in her side yard, holding the dripping hose and shaking her head. "Robert Reynolds," she said, "there's a hole the size of a small boy in my *other* boxwood bush." Robert looked at the hole he had left when he tried to leap over the bush on his way to see Ashley.

"You're absolutely right," said Robert. "That *is* a big hole." When Mrs. Snead turned around, Robert sizzled at her, but not for long.

Then he headed up the sidewalk toward home.

Breinigsville, PA USA
08 November 2010
248929BV00001B/80/P